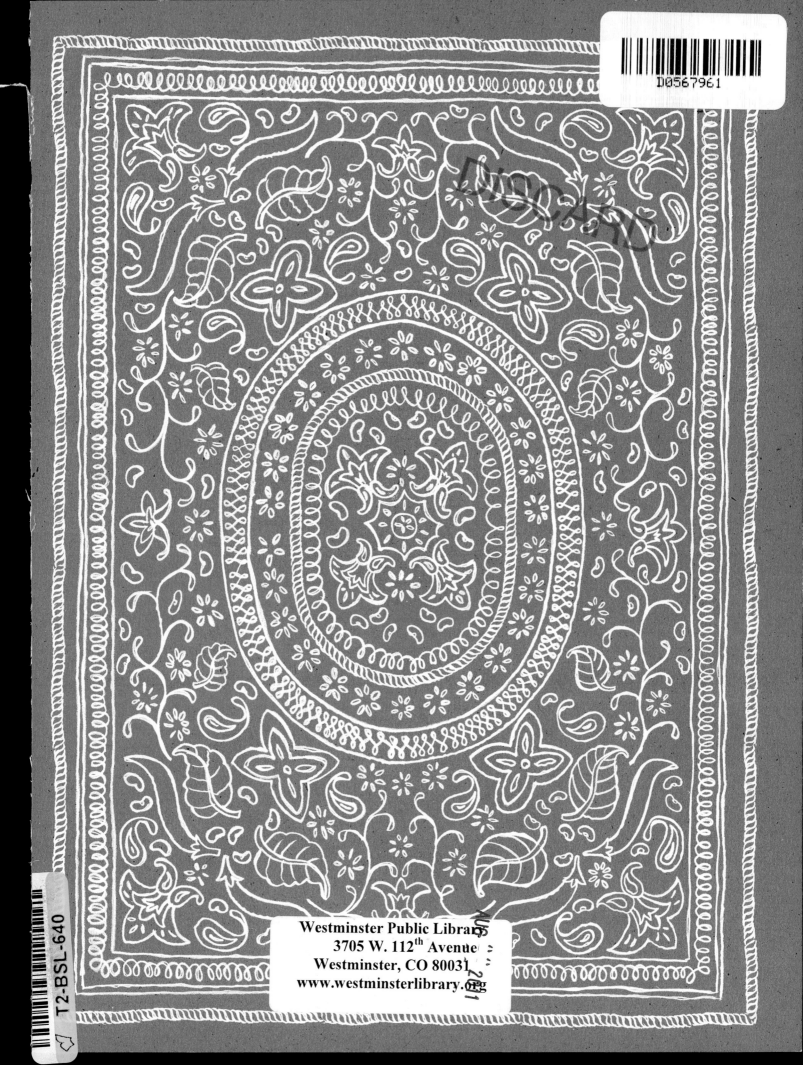

For all those in the world who share with others,
and for my editor, Meredith Mundy.
—D. D.

For Simonne,
the prettiest gal this side of Skinflint.
—B. G.

STERLING and the distinctive Sterling logo
are registered trademarks of Sterling Publishing Co., Inc.

**Library of Congress Cataloging-in-Publication Data**
Davis, David, 1948 Oct. 29–
Fandango stew / by David Davis ; illustrated by Ben Galbraith.
p. cm.
Summary: Penniless Slim and his grandson Luis ride into the unwelcoming western town of Skinflint,
and manage to rustle up a delicious meal for all its citizens out of one lone bean.
ISBN 978-1-4027-6527-8
[1. Folklore.] I. Galbraith, Ben, ill. II. Stone soup. English. III. Title.
PZ8.1.D2887Fan 2011
398.2—dc22
[E]
2010004775

Lot#:
2  4  6  8  10  9  7  5  3  1
11/10

Published by Sterling Publishing Co., Inc. 387 Park Avenue South, New York, NY 10016.
Text © 2011 by David Davis. Illustrations © 2011 by Ben Galbraith.
Distributed in Canada by Sterling Publishing.
c/o Canadian Manda Group, 165 Dufferin Street, Toronto, Ontario, Canada M6K 3H6
Distributed in the United Kingdom by GMC Distribution Services, Castle Place, 166 High Street, Lewes, East Sussex, England BN7 1XU
Distributed in Australia by Capricorn Link (Australia) Pty. Ltd. P.O. Box 704, Windsor, NSW 2756, Australia

*Printed in China. All rights reserved.*

Sterling ISBN 978-1-4027-6527-8

For information about custom editions, special sales, premium and corporate purchases, please contact
Sterling Special Sales Department at 800-805-5489 or specialsales@sterlingpublishing.com.

The artwork for this book was created using a mixture of oil paints, found objects, and digitally scanned textures.

Designed by Katrina Damkoehler

# FANDANGO STEW

by **DAVID DAVIS**

illustrated by **BEN GALBRAITH**

STERLING

New York / London

**S**lim rubbed his grumbling belly as he rode into the town of Skinflint. "I'm so hungry I could eat a boiled leather boot," he said to his grandson, Luis.

"Neither of us has a peso, *Abuelo*," said Luis. "Looks like fandango stew for supper again."

Slim grinned and sang,

**"Chili's good, so is barbecue,
but nothing's FINER than**

**FANDANGO STEW!"**

When they stopped to water their mustangs,
the town sheriff collared them.

"You two cowpokes can just keep right on a-riding," said the sheriff. "The hard-working citizens of Skinflint don't feed saddle tramps. It ain't far to the city limits, and it's downhill all the way."

"We're not aiming to lasso a handout," said Slim.
"My grandson and I rode in to treat Skinflint to a pot
of fandango bean stew."

The sheriff narrowed his eyes. "I've
never heard tell of a fandango bean!"

Slim pulled a small bean from his vest pocket and held it up in the air.
He sang,

# "Chili's good, so is barbecue,
## but nothing's FINER than
# FANDANGO STEW!"

"What are you sidewinders trying to pull?" growled the sheriff.

The mayor moseyed over with the owner of the general store. Both men laughed. They said, "You skunks can't make stew for the whole town with one bean."

"Lend us that big iron kettle yonder and you'll see," said Slim.

"These *hombres* are *loco*," said the shopkeeper. "But I want to see this."

The sheriff twirled his mustache. "Well, I guess it won't hurt anything to watch two fools boil water." He and the blacksmith rolled the huge iron pot into the town square.

Slim built a fire under it while Luis filled it up with water. When the pot boiled, Luis kissed the tiny fandango bean and dropped it in. Slim and Luis sang in two-part harmony,

## "Chili's good, so is barbecue, but nothing's FINER than FANDANGO STEW!"

The bank president poked his head out the bank window and yelled,

"What's that

ruckus

going on

out there?"

The mayor pointed into the pot. "Why, it's the nearest next-to-nothing you ever saw!"

Slim ignored them and stirred the pot with a long wooden spoon. "This stew is *muy bueno*," he said. "But, if we added a little salt and pepper to season the fandango bean, it would be truly *magnifico*."

The banker chuckled. "Shucks, I can lend you a little salt and pepper."

He shut the window, ran outside with two fancy gold salt and pepper shakers, and sprinkled the seasonings into the pot.

Then, Slim, Luis, and the banker sang in three-part harmony,

# "Chili's good, so is barbecue,
## but nothing's FINER than
## FANDANGO STEW!"

Slim tasted the stew and sighed.

"What's ailing you?" asked the blacksmith.

"Nothing," said Slim. "I was just a-thinking how a purple onion would bring out the flavor of the fandango bean."

"I guess the wife and I could rustle up an onion," the blacksmith said. His wife fetched one and the blacksmith diced it to toss into the boiling water.

Then, Slim, Luis, the banker, the blacksmith, and his wife sang, in five-part harmony,

**"Chili's good, so is barbecue, but nothing's FINER than FANDANGO STEW!"**

Luis sniffed the air and said,
"This stew smells good, *muchachos*.
Not as tasty as that batch over in
Dog Leg Gulch—but good."

"It can't be helped, *amigo*," Slim said.
"We had potatoes in Dog Leg Gulch.
This is Skinflint."

A lawyer in a frock coat elbowed his way up to the kettle. "We've got passels of potatoes!" he yelled. He disappeared and returned wheeling a huge barrow of spuds. "Skinflint has more potatoes than Dog Leg Gulch—case closed!"

While they peeled potatoes, Slim, Luis, the banker, the blacksmith, his wife, and the lawyer were merry. They sang in six-part harmony,

## "Chili's good,
### so is barbecue,
### but nothing's FINER than

# FANDANGO STEW!"

Skinflint's pretty school teacher tugged at Slim's arm. She opened a large cookbook. "Pardon me, sir, but it says here that you need more than potatoes for a healthful stew. Children need vegetables!"

"You're right as rain, ma'am. If this was the stew we cooked in New Summerfield, we'd have plenty," Slim said. "They grow lots of vegetables there—but Skinflint is just a one-horse town."

"One-horse town!" yelled the sheriff. "Dag nab it, I'll show you vegetables!" He whistled up his deputies. "Boys, make tracks to my garden. Pick anything that even *looks* like a vegetable. Pronto! Even pick the okra!" In a few minutes they returned with baskets loaded with peppers, peas, cabbage, asparagus, squash, carrots, and okra.

Slim winked at Luis, and said, "Sheriff, perhaps you brought too many vegetables. They might smother the delicate flavor of the fandango bean."

"Listen, pilgrim—you'll add all those vegetables, and like it. Or you'll spend the night in the jailhouse!" the sheriff growled.

"If you insist," said Slim.

The teacher and the schoolchildren washed the vegetables at the town pump. Luis added all of them to the stew—even the okra. Just then, the Skinflint Culture Club ladies strutted over, twirling their parasols. Not to be outdone, they stirred in five pounds of brown rice and a bushel of prize-winning heirloom tomatoes. They had their men folk set up tables and hang paper lanterns all around the square.

Then, Slim, Luis, the banker, the blacksmith, his wife, the lawyer, the mayor, the deputies, the Ladies Culture Club, their men folk, the school teacher, and the children sang in forty-seven-part harmony,

## "Chili's good, so is barbecue,

## but nothing's FINER than
## FANDANGO STEW!"

The stew simmered and the aroma drifted over the whole town.

When the fandango stew was done, the storekeeper and his wife served it with big glasses of sweet tea. Everybody had all the stew they wanted. Nobody ate more than the sheriff. He even took bowls of stew to the *desperados* in the jailhouse.

After supper the mayor burped and said, "Fellers, I'm as full as a tick." He clapped Slim and Luis on the back. "Now, tell me if this isn't the best dang stew shindig you buckaroos ever saw!"

"It is truly a fine *fiesta*," said Luis.

"I've never seen better," said Slim.

When night fell, the moon rose over Skinflint like a big yellow balloon. Everyone strolled home, all tuckered out from the excitement—and nobody went to bed hungry.

The next morning, the whole town turned out to say good-bye to Slim and Luis. The mayor dabbed his teary eyes with a handkerchief. He said, "We sure wish you galoots would stay a spell."

COURTHOUSE

SCHOOL

"We'd best be hitting the trail," Slim said as they mounted up.

"Before you go," the shopkeeper said, "tell me where I can get some of those fandango beans."

Luis pointed to the barrel on the porch. "You've got plenty right there, *amigo*."

"Why, those are just common pinto beans!" the shopkeeper's wife replied.

"Any bean makes a fine fandango stew," Slim said. "Just add generosity and kindness."

"Well, hog-tie me with a noodle," laughed the sheriff.

Slim and Luis tipped their hats, and the whole town could hear their fine duet as they rode into the sunrise . . .

"Chili's good, so is barbecue,
but nothing's FINER than

FANDANGO STEW!"

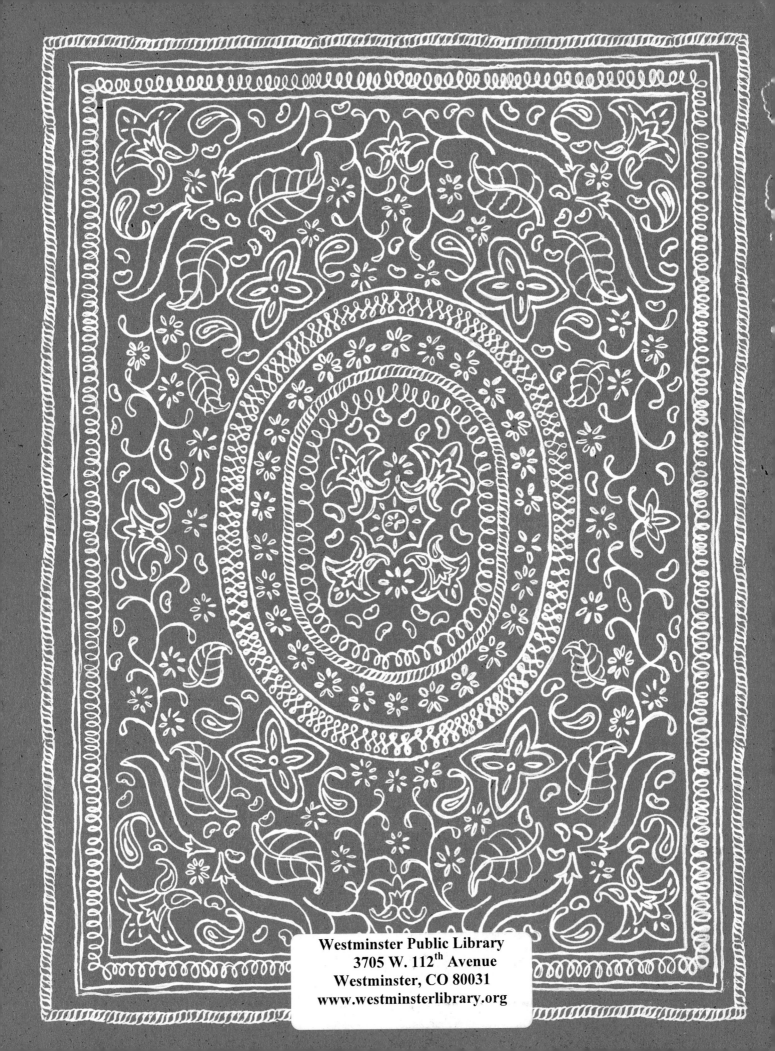